Icinori

ISSUN BÔSHI

-The One-Inch Boy-

LITTLE
GESTALTEN

Once, in a country far away,
there lived a peasant farmer and his wife.
They had no children and every day, to lift their spirits
on the walk to and from the fields, they sang:
"We'd like a little boy, any size at all.
We'd like him little, we'd like him small.
We'd love him tiniest of all."

A miracle happened.
They had a child.
But—and this hardly came as a surprise—
he really was tiny.
And they called him Issun Bôshi,
"the One-Inch Boy."

The years passed and Issun Bôshi became nimble and smart.
He learned to dance, he learned to sing,
and the country folk came to see the charming way
he moved his little body.
A hardworking boy, he helped his parents in the fields,
and they repaid him richly in love and gratitude.

By the age of fifteen,
there was no denying it:
he still hadn't grown;
not an inch,
not one tiny little bit.

One day, Issun Bôshi went to his parents and said to them:
"I have decided to go in search of adventure.
The world is big, especially for me.
In the city, I will find a life that suits me well."
His parents were much moved. His mother gave him a rice bowl,
which he carried on his shoulders, and his father presented him
with a beautiful needle, which he wore at his belt.
Thus equipped, he was ready to go. And off he went.

The world is so big
and Issun Bôshi so small.

While Issun Bôshi was gathering twigs in the forest to make
a fire, all of a sudden, at a bend in the path, he came across a
strange-smelling, strange-looking creature, like none he had
ever seen before: gigantic, hairy, and misshapen.
The creature spoke:
"Ti-Ki-Ki! Who are you?"
The little man was not afraid and answered:
"I am Issun Bôshi, the One-Inch Boy."
"Ti-Ki-Ki!" said the ogre, hopping from one foot to the other.
"I'll make you a deal.
If you follow this stream, you will come to a city.
In this city, you will see the grand house of a nobleman.
In this house, you will find a beautiful treasure.
And Ti-Ki-Ki, you'll bring it to me! Then, my magic hammer
Uchide-no-Kozuchi, 'He Who Grants Wishes,'
will reward you with the height your parents forgot to give you.
What do you say?"

Quick-witted and honest, Issun replied:
"I shall go and see this city, I shall go and see this nobleman,
but he'll keep his treasure, you'll keep your hammer,
and I'll keep my tiny size. That way, we'll be quits.
Good day to you, I must be on my way."
On board his bowl, sailing towards the city, Issun Bôshi thought
he could still hear the ogre's voice in the distance, like an echo:
"Ti-Ki-Ki! Ti-Ki-Ki! Ti-Ki-Ki!"

Finally, Issun Bôshi arrived in the city. What a commotion!
Traders, horses, snakes, carts, men, birds, women, fruit, children;
hustle and bustle all over the place: people running,
people shouting, all of them nearly crushing little Bôshi.
And swiftly, with all his agility, he threaded his way through the
crowd, hopping and skipping between all the legs and feet.

Issun Bôshi found a grand house,
as beautiful as can be, and began to shout:
"Give me a job, I want to work!"
Roused by the noise, the whole household came running
and was astonished to discover the origin of this strange din:
a tiny little man, no more than an inch high.
"What good could you possibly be to me, you little pipsqueak?"
the nobleman asked, looking down from his balcony.
And Issun Bôshi began to sing.
And Issun Bôshi began to dance.
Soon, the whole neighborhood was watching the spectacle
and the crowd laughed, whistled, and clapped.

Then a young girl appeared and cried out:
"Papa, I'm bored!
Give me this little person, I beg you, he can read to me,
sing me songs, and keep me company."
Exhausted by all the hubbub, the nobleman gave in to
his daughter and hired Issun Bôshi.

From then on, Issun Bôshi accompanied the girl wherever she went.
One day he would sing, the next he would dance.
Time passed and he worked hard at inventing tricks and songs
to entertain his young mistress.
And she was delighted to have a doll that could read and think.
But the little man began to say to himself that it might be nice,
just once, to be, not really bigger, but perhaps a little bit less tiny,
so that she would view him differently, especially because she was
very beautiful.

One day, out walking in the forest, Issun Bôshi was amusing
the young girl by acting out the battle between the ant and the
caterpillar. All of a sudden, the strange-smelling, strange-looking
ogre appeared:
"Ti-Ki-Ki! Thank you, Bôshi Bôshi, at last you have brought me
the treasure I asked you for. A thousand thanks, my little one!"
And with these words, he put the young girl under his arm
and rushed off as fast as his legs would carry him.

A quick runner, Issun Bôshi soon
caught up with them, leapt,
gripped on tightly to the ogre,
and bit him with all his might.
Infuriated by this pesky midget,
the ogre swallowed him whole.

Deep down in the ogre's stomach, Issun Bôshi felt a
terrible anger rising within him. He seized the needle
at his belt and plunged it into the giant's insides:
he stabbed and slashed and stabbed again,
like a hornet, like a wasp.
Nothing escaped him, neither the liver, nor the kidneys,
nor the heart, nor even the throat, so much so that
the monster, doubled up with pain, spat him out again.

Straight away, as quick as a flash, Issun grabbed the ogre's magic
hammer, *Uchide no Kozuchi,* "He Who Grants Wishes."
While the young girl and the ogre looked on in amazement,
little Bôshi grew and grew and grew.
The "One-Inch Boy" turned into a man who was tall and strong and,
above all, terribly angry.
Without his hammer, the ogre took fright and scurried off, whining:
"Teh-Keh-Keh! Teh-Keh-Keh! Teh-Keh-Keh!"

People say he can still be seen walking in the depths of the forest,
a little tiny ogre, nibbling grass to soothe his punctured insides.
People say that Issun Bôshi sometimes misses being small,
and that he still treasures his bowl and needle.
People say that the nobleman's daughter has taken a different view
of Issun Bôshi and that their story is not yet over.